W9-AQS-909

WITHDRAWN

11/16

Dear Parents and Educators,

Welcome to Penguin Young Readers! As parents and educators, you know that each child develops at his or her own pace—in terms of speech, critical thinking, and, of course, reading. Penguin Young Readers recognizes this fact. As a result, each Penguin Young Readers book is assigned a traditional easy-to-read level (1–4) as well as a Guided Reading Level (A–P). Both of these systems will help you choose the right book for your child. Please refer to the back of each book for specific leveling information. Penguin Young Readers features esteemed authors and illustrators, stories about favorite characters, fascinating nonfiction, and more!

What Does Otis See?

LEVEL 1

GUIDED
READING
LEVEL **C**

This book is perfect for an **Emergent Reader** who:
• can read in a left-to-right and top-to-bottom progression;
• can recognize some beginning and ending letter sounds;
• can use picture clues to help tell the story; and
• can understand the basic plot and sequence of simple stories.

Here are some **activities** you can do during and after reading this book:
• Making Predictions: Sometimes pictures contain clues in them that help you guess what will happen next. On each spread there is a clue about what animal Otis will see next. Have the child go through, find the clues, and try to guess what animal is coming!
• Read the Pictures: Use the pictures to tell the story. Have the child go through the book, retelling the story just by looking at the pictures.

Remember, sharing the love of reading with a child is the best gift you can give!

—Bonnie Bader, EdM
  Penguin Young Readers program

*Penguin Young Readers are leveled by independent reviewers applying the standards developed by Irene Fountas and Gay Su Pinnell in *Matching Books to Readers: Using Leveled Books in Guided Reading*, Heinemann, 1999.

PENGUIN YOUNG READERS
An Imprint of Penguin Random House LLC

Penguin supports copyright. Copyright fuels creativity, encourages diverse voices,
promotes free speech, and creates a vibrant culture. Thank you for buying an authorized edition of this
book and for complying with copyright laws by not reproducing, scanning, or distributing any part of it
in any form without permission. You are supporting writers and allowing Penguin to continue to publish
books for every reader.

Text copyright © 2015 by Loren Long. Illustrations copyright © 2009, 2011, 2013 by Loren Long.
All rights reserved. Published by Penguin Young Readers, an imprint of Penguin Random House LLC,
345 Hudson Street, New York, New York 10014.
Manufactured in China.

Library of Congress Cataloging-in-Publication Data is available.

ISBN 978-0-448-48758-8 (pbk)   10 9 8 7 6 5 4 3 2 1
ISBN 978-0-448-48759-5 (hc)   10 9 8 7 6 5 4 3 2 1

FROM #1 NEW YORK TIMES BESTSELLER LOREN LONG

What Does Otis See?

by Loren Long

Penguin Young Readers
An Imprint of Penguin Random House

This is Otis.

He is a tractor.

He lives on a farm.

There is a lot to see.

What does Otis see?

Otis sees a calf.

12

What does Otis see?

Otis sees a horse.

What does Otis see?

Otis sees a bull.

What does Otis see?

Otis sees ducks.

What does Otis see?

Otis sees a puppy.

What does Otis see?

Otis sees friends!